HEROIN
AFFECTING LIVES

BY CLARA MacCARALD

MOMENTUM

Published by The Child's World®
1980 Lookout Drive • Mankato, MN 56003-1705
800-599-READ • www.childsworld.com

ISBN 9781503844919 (Reinforced Library Binding)
ISBN 9781503846425 (Portable Document Format)
ISBN 9781503847613 (Online Multi-user eBook)
LCCN 2019957702

Printed in the United States of America

Some names and details have been changed
throughout this book to protect privacy.

CONTENTS

MOMENTUM

FAST FACTS

What It Is

▶ Heroin is an illegal **opioid** drug made from opium poppy plants. The drug can be white, brown, or black.

▶ Heroin might be mixed with other things.

How It's Used

▶ Someone can **inject** heroin into his or her body.

▶ Someone can snort, sniff, or smoke heroin.

Physical Effects

▶ Heroin can make people feel sleepy or sick. Their skin might feel warm, their mouth dry, and their legs and arms heavy. The drug can slow down a person's breathing.

▶ A heroin **overdose** can make a person fall into a deep sleep or even die.

Mental Effects

▶ People might experience a **euphoric** feeling called being high.

▶ People who use heroin are highly likely to become **addicted** to the drug.

Heroin Use and Deaths (2014–2017)

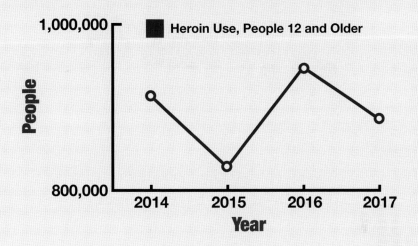

Heroin Use, People 12 and Older

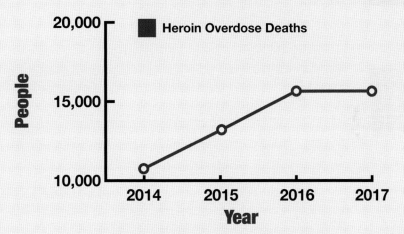

Heroin Overdose Deaths

"Overdose Death Rates." *National Institute on Drug Abuse*, 29 Jan. 2019, drugabuse.gov. Accessed 26 Nov. 2019.

While the number of people using heroin in the United States did not change much between 2014 and 2017, the number of deaths rose. Heroin is becoming deadlier. Many of the people who died took heroin with fentanyl added. Fentanyl is an extremely powerful human-made opioid. Its strength makes overdosing more likely.

CHAPTER ONE

A TERRIBLE LOSS

One day, 18-year-old Andy told his parents he needed to talk to them about something. Worried, his parents followed him to the living room. A fire crackled in the fireplace. Andy's medals and prizes decorated the walls. He used to be a star on the track team. But he had stopped going to practice. He no longer enjoyed playing piano or biking.

Andy's parents sat next to each other on the sofa and took a good look at him. Instead of being healthy and strong like before, Andy was weak. His clothes hung from his skinny body. What had caused him to change so much?

Andy took a deep breath. He told his parents he had become addicted to heroin. His parents were upset, but they asked him to go on.

◄ Sometimes, people are prescribed opioids to help with pain. They can develop an unhealthy dependency if they take too many.

Like many people who use heroin, Andy had first been **prescribed** opioids. It started two years ago, after he had major work done on his teeth. The doctor gave him a prescription for opioids. Prescription opioids are legal painkillers, but they are also strong and addictive. They have similar effects on the brain as heroin does. When the medicine ran out, Andy felt very sick. His body had gotten used to having opioids.

That weekend, one of his friends had some heroin. Andy tried smoking the drug. Andy liked the euphoric feeling he got from heroin at first. He began getting high every weekend. During the week, he went into **withdrawal**. People in withdrawal from heroin can feel nervous and upset. They might sweat a lot and their bodies might ache. Sometimes, although rarely, heroin withdrawal can kill someone.

Withdrawal made it hard for Andy to do anything else. Andy's life had become all about how to get the next dose of heroin. He was tired of living like that. He wanted to stop. But he couldn't stop by himself. That's when he told his parents he needed to talk to them about his drug use.

Andy's parents helped him get into **rehab**. One week later, Andy moved to a rehab center. He lived there for nine months. At rehab, people are kept away from drugs. They talk to doctors.

People who are in withdrawal tend ▶ to feel sick and anxious.

They discuss how to change their risky drug habits. But when Andy came back home, his friends were still doing heroin. Soon, he was doing heroin again.

Andy tried rehab two more times. He told his mother that someday he wanted to help others stay away from drugs. He would go into schools and share his story with kids.

At 21, Andy was finally doing better. He hadn't used heroin for several months. He applied to a community college and got in.

After Andy's first class, he left the building. He walked across the school grounds to where he had parked. It was a beautiful fall day. Many leaves were turning colors.

GETTING HELP

If you or someone you know needs help dealing with drug dependency, you can start by talking with your parents or your doctor. They can help you decide where you or your friend can get treated. If you don't feel comfortable talking with people you know, you can call the Substance Abuse and Mental Health Services Administration at 1-800-662-4357. People on the other end can connect you with help. If you need to speak to someone right away, call the National Suicide Prevention Lifeline at 1-800-273-8255. If you think someone has overdosed on heroin, call 911.

▲ **In rehab, people can get help with their drug habits from professionals and peers.**

He got into his car. He still had a small amount of heroin inside. Andy still longed for the drug even though he hated it. No one saw him get into his car. Surely, he could do heroin just one more time. No one ever needed to know.

Andy smoked the heroin. Because he hadn't used the drug in so long, his body wasn't used to it anymore. The heroin killed him.

Andy's mother missed her son terribly. She wanted to do something in memory of Andy, so she started a yearly race. The race raised money to help other young people struggling with drug use.

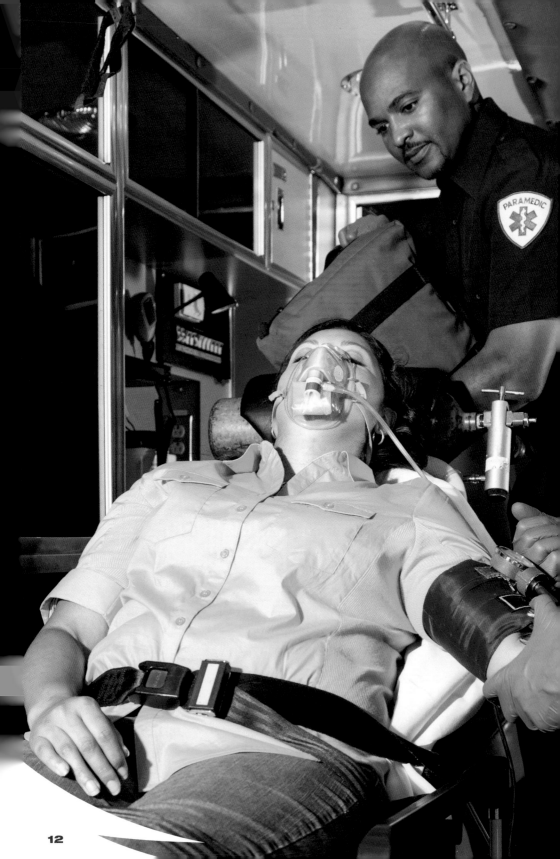

CHAPTER TWO

SAVING LIVES

Helen, a **paramedic**, started the ambulance. She and Brian, another paramedic, had just dropped off a woman at the hospital. The woman had almost died from using heroin. The paramedics had saved her life with Narcan, a drug which can stop an opioid overdose. She was not the first person they'd seen who had overdosed. She would not be the last, either. Their local area was suffering from an opioid **epidemic**.

A call came over the radio. A man was lying on the ground at a soccer practice field. Brian and Helen shared a look. Maybe it wasn't a person using drugs. Maybe he was sick or had hurt himself.

The ambulance sped toward the address, lights flashing. Helen pulled into a parking lot. A man lay by the bleachers.

◄ **Paramedics are trained to help people in emergencies.**

In the field, girls sat and cried, their soccer balls forgotten. Parents tried to move them away.

Brian grabbed a bag of gear, and the paramedics jogged toward the fallen man. The man's lips were turning a blue color the paramedics knew all too well. He had overdosed on an opioid. The drug was shutting down his breathing. The blue color had come from a lack of oxygen.

The paramedics got to work. Helen dug through the bag and pulled out a container of Narcan. Brian sprayed the medicine in the man's nose. The man was breathing, but very slowly.

THE OPIOID EPIDEMIC

Beginning in the late 1990s, doctors gave out increasing numbers of prescription opioids for pain relief. Many people became addicted. Some people began misusing prescription opioids, and some started to use heroin. In 2017, an estimated 2.1 million people aged 12 or older used opioids in an unhealthy way, while 652,000 used heroin. About 47,000 Americans died of an opioid overdose that year. The U.S. Department of Health and Human Services stated that the opioid epidemic was a public health emergency. Public health emergencies can also happen when too many people die from the flu or other diseases.

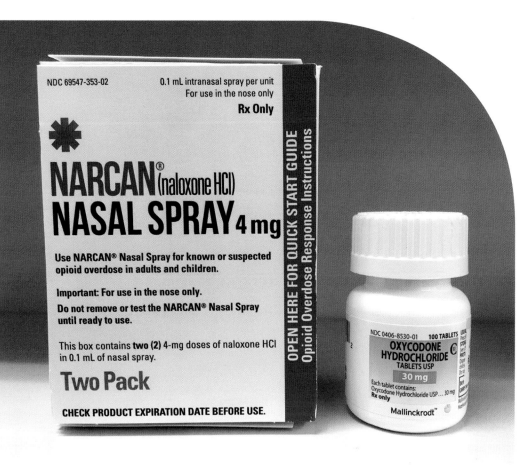

▲ **Narcan can reverse the effects of an overdose.**

The paramedics checked him over and found his heart was beating slowly as well. The paramedics put a mask over his face and pumped air into his mouth.

A girl came up to them. She was the man's daughter. In tears, she asked why her father didn't wake up. The paramedics said they would do everything they could to help him. Helen pulled the mask away and Brian gave the man another dose of Narcan. The man opened his eyes. He was awake.

He rose suddenly, and the paramedics jumped out of the way as the man threw up. Narcan had blocked his body from using the opioid he had taken in. Now he was in withdrawal.

When the man could talk, Brian and Helen knelt next to him. They asked if he had used heroin. The man admitted that he had. He felt sorry for messing up by taking heroin, especially at his daughter's soccer practice, where children were nearby.

As the paramedics began to pack their bags, the sound of a police car pulling into the parking lot made them look up. Two officers got out and strode towards the scene. Someone had called them because the man had used heroin. The man's daughter would probably be taken away from him.

When the paramedics left the man at the hospital, they wondered if they would see him again. Even overdosing doesn't stop a person with an addiction from seeking the high that comes from using heroin. Sometimes Helen and Brian saw the same person overdose several times in a row. They wished they could stop more people from using heroin, but for now they would keep saving lives.

Parents who are arrested for drug use may have ▶ their children taken away from them by a court.

CHAPTER THREE

BAD NEWS

L isa approached the brick building. In her purse were several dirty needles. A few hours ago, Lisa had used one of those needles to inject heroin. Her skin still felt hot and she was having trouble thinking straight. But she remembered hearing about the needle exchange at the city health department. The city knew it couldn't stop all people from using drugs. But it could give people clean needles. Then people could at least avoid getting diseases from dirty needles.

She entered the office and joined the other people that were sitting by the front desk. They all had come to exchange dirty needles for clean ones. Lisa often borrowed dirty needles. Each dirty needle had already gone into another person's vein. Certain illnesses are found in the blood. Someone with **HIV** could pass the disease to another person.

◄ **Dirty needles can spread diseases. Doctors give out clean needles.**

Some users hid their dirty needles outdoors, such as in a park. They didn't want the police to find the needles. Members of the public came across used needles. The needles put people in danger of catching a disease. The city had started the needle exchange to remove dirty needles from the local community.

Lisa filled out some papers. A staff member named Sarah took her into the back room. Sarah had Lisa put her dirty needles into a plastic box. The box would keep the needles from poking anyone by mistake.

Sarah handed Lisa a pack of as many clean needles as Lisa thought she'd use for the week. Sarah explained how to inject heroin as safely as possible. Even without sharing needles, people who use heroin could still pick up nasty bacteria and harm their own veins.

Sarah had such a kind smile. She asked how Lisa was doing. Tears came to Lisa's eyes. Sometimes Lisa felt like no one cared about her anymore. She didn't want to keep using heroin, but she was addicted. Her attempts to stop hadn't worked yet. Her family didn't speak to her because of her drug use. She lost her job and her home. Now she was staying with a friend who also did heroin.

Sarah told Lisa the needle exchange offered other services. Lisa had trouble following everything Sarah said, but she agreed to take an HIV test. Sarah put on plastic gloves to protect herself.

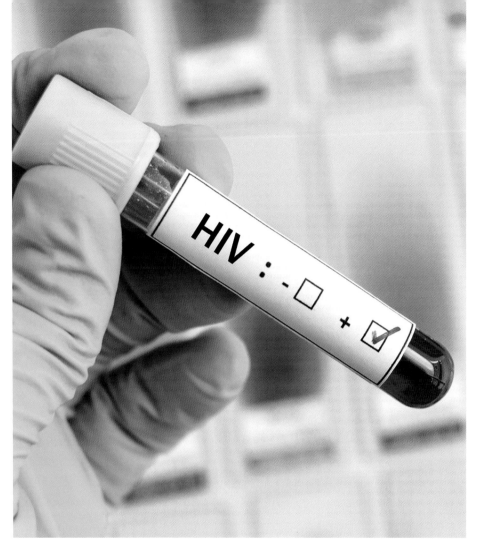

▲ **Doctors can test people for HIV. Someone with HIV can get therapy to slow down the disease's effects.**

She poked Lisa's finger. A small drop of blood welled up. Sarah drew the blood up into a tube to test it. In ten minutes, the test would tell if Lisa had the virus.

Sarah talked more while they waited. Lisa tried to listen, but she was nervous. Finally, the results came back. Lisa had HIV.

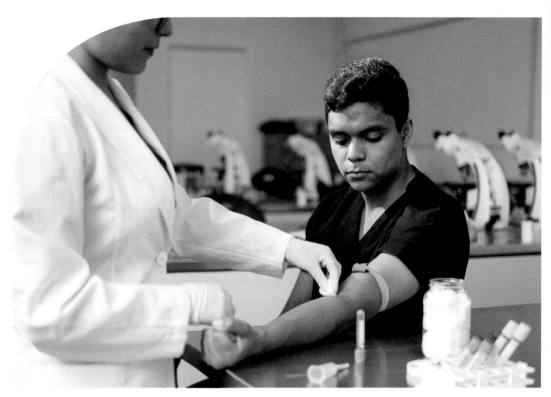

▲ **People can get their blood tested for diseases at needle exchanges.**

Lisa sat back, stunned. There was no cure. And HIV can lead to a deadly disease called AIDS. AIDS attacks the immune system, which is the system of the body that guards a person from other sicknesses.

Sarah told Lisa that people at the needle exchange could help her find a doctor. If she treated the HIV, she'd be less likely to get AIDS. Sarah also told Lisa where she could find treatment for drug addiction. Now Lisa could start taking better care of herself.

The red ribbon is a symbol that promotes ▶ awareness for people living with AIDS.

CHAPTER FOUR

TURNING AROUND

Police lights flashed in Kelsey's rearview mirror. She'd been drifting in and out of her lane as she drove to visit a friend. At first, she struggled to remember what to do. Then she remembered the police wanted her to stop. Stones crunched under her wheels as she pulled to the side of the road.

Kelsey gripped the steering wheel as an officer walked toward her car. Would he know she had used heroin? He knocked on the window and she rolled it down. She tried to smile up at him.

The officer asked her a few questions, but she had trouble understanding his words. She lied and said she was very tired. Frowning, he told her to get out of her car and into the back of the police car. Kelsey was in no state to drive.

Once she was in the police car, the officer asked if someone could come get her. Kelsey gave him her mom's phone number.

◄ **Driving while on drugs can be extremely dangerous.**

▲ When police search cars, they might use dogs to sniff out drugs.

The officer returned to Kelsey's car. The way Kelsey was acting made him guess she had drugs inside the car, which gave him the right to search it.

Kelsey started to worry. Her mom didn't know she used heroin. She didn't want to let her mom down. As her mom drove up with Kelsey's little brother in the back, the officer stepped out of Kelsey's car. He held up a bag containing powdered heroin.

▲ People who are caught with heroin may go to jail for a few nights or much longer.

Kelsey watched her mom talk to the police officer. Her mom looked scared.

Kelsey spent a few days in jail. When she got out, she couldn't stop using heroin. As time went on, Kelsey needed more money to buy the drug. She stole things from her mom's house, such as a necklace passed down from her grandmother. Her mom took away Kelsey's car keys so Kelsey wouldn't sell her car. Kelsey's mom started locking up her money and anything expensive. She told Kelsey that Kelsey needed help before she ended up back in jail. Kelsey agreed to go into rehab.

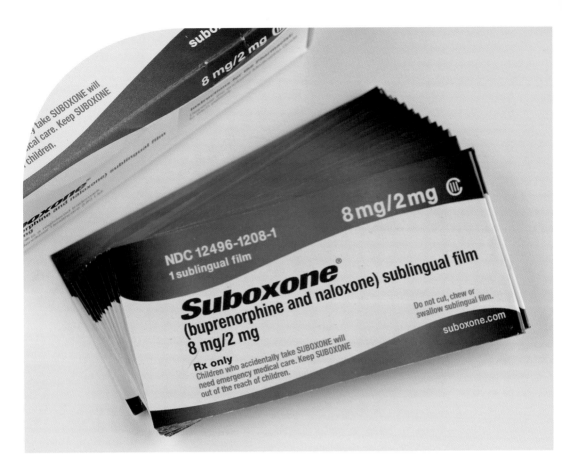

▲ Suboxone helps people not crave heroin as much.

One of the things Kelsey did in rehab was start taking a medicine called Suboxone. Every day, she melted a strip of Suboxone under her tongue. The medicine gave her a weak high, but it reduced her need for heroin. It helped her stay away from the drug.

Months later, Kelsey was out of rehab. She and her brother were hanging out in the backyard. Kelsey had a new phone. She was texting with her friend, who'd started speaking to her again.

Her mom stepped out of the house and called her name. Kelsey looked up. Had she done something wrong?

Her mom held out a set of keys, smiling. For months, Kelsey's mom had kept her from driving in case she might buy drugs or try to sell the car. But now Kelsey's mom asked if she wanted to take her brother to see a movie.

Kelsey slowly took the keys. Did her mom really trust her? Her mom nodded.

Kelsey smiled and gave her mom a huge hug. She and her brother raced to the car. That night, she and her brother had so much fun laughing at the movie that she didn't miss heroin at all.

THINK ABOUT IT

▶ Why would a person go into rehab instead of trying to quit heroin by themselves?
▶ Using heroin can ruin people's relationships and even lead to death. Why do you think so many people start using this drug?
▶ Why would needle exchanges offer testing for HIV/AIDS?

GLOSSARY

addicted (uh-DIK-tid): Someone who is addicted to something cannot give up using or doing that thing. People who use heroin can become addicted to the drug.

epidemic (ep-i-DEM-ik): An epidemic is an illness or other problem which is found widely in a community. The U.S. government is worried about an epidemic of opioid use.

euphoric (yoo-FOR-ik): Euphoric means a strong feeling of excitement and happiness. People like the euphoric feeling heroin causes.

HIV: HIV is a virus which affects the immune system and causes AIDS. Doctors use medicine to treat people with HIV.

inject (in-JEKT): To inject is to put something into one's body using a needle. People can harm their blood vessels when they inject heroin.

opioid (OH-pee-oyd): An opioid drug belongs to a class of drugs which relieve pain and relax the body. Heroin is an opioid drug.

overdose (OH-vur-dohss): An overdose is a dose of a drug which is too large and may either make a person sick or kill them. People may overdose on even small amounts of heroin.

paramedic (par-uh-MED-ik): A paramedic is someone trained to treat medical problems who is not a doctor. A paramedic might save someone's life.

prescribed (pri-SKRIBED): When a doctor has prescribed a medication, she has written a note that allows a patient to receive a given treatment. Opioids are often prescribed for pain.

rehab (REE-hab): Rehab is a type of treatment for drug abuse. Most rehab centers have strict rules for patients.

withdrawal (with-DRAW-uhl): Withdrawal is the experience of physical and mental effects when a person stops taking a drug. Withdrawal makes it hard for people to quit heroin.

TO LEARN MORE

BOOKS

Hamen, Susan E. *Heroin and Its Dangers*.
San Diego, CA: ReferencePoint Press, 2020.

Marcovitz, Hal. *The Opioid Epidemic*.
San Diego, CA: ReferencePoint Press, 2018.

Marsico, Katie. *Heroin*. New York, NY: Marshall Cavendish, 2014.

Paris, Stephanie Herweck. *Drugs and Alcohol*.
Huntington Beach, CA: Teacher Created Materials, 2013.

WEBSITES

Visit our website for links about addiction to heroin: **childsworld.com/links**

*Note to Parents, Teachers, and Librarians: We routinely verify our Web links to make
sure they are safe and active sites. So encourage your readers to check them out!*

SELECTED BIBLIOGRAPHY

"Buprenorphine." *Substance Abuse and Mental Health Services
Administration*, 7 May 2019, samhsa.gov. Accessed 19 Dec. 2019.

Darke, Shane, et al. "Yes, People Can Die from Opiate Withdrawal."
National Drug and Alcohol Research Centre, 30 August 2019,
ndarc.med.unsw.edu.au. Accessed 19 Dec. 2019.

"Why Does Heroin Use Create Special Risk for Contracting
HIV/AIDS and Hepatitis B and C?" *National Institute on Drug
Abuse*, June 2018, drugabuse.gov. Accessed 19 Dec. 2019.

INDEX

ABOUT THE AUTHOR

Clara MacCarald is a freelance writer with a master's degree in biology. She lives with her family in an off-grid house nestled in the forests of central New York. When not parenting her daughter, she spends her time writing nonfiction books for kids.